To my three sons, our Mother, and the entire Marley Massive...
thanks for always being there —C. M.

To G. H., I know that with you every little thing is going to be
all right! For my family and friends: R. N., C. C., Y. P., E. B., I., L. H.
With all my love. —V. B. N.

Text © 2012 by Cedella Marley.
Story adapted from the "Three Little Birds" lyrics written by Bob Marley.
Published by Blue Mountain Music Ltd/Irish Town Songs (ASCAP)
o/b/o Fifty-Six Hope Road Music Ltd, and Blackwell Fuller Music Publishing LLC.
Illustrations © 2012 by Vanessa Brantley-Newton.
Pages 7 and 23 photograph of Bob Marley by Adrian Boot © Fifty-Six Music, Ltd.

Library of Congress Cataloging-in-Publication Data
Marley, Cedella.
Every little thing / by Cedella Marley ; illustrated by Vanessa Brantley-Newton.
p. cm.
"Based on the song by Bob Marley."
Summary: In this illustrated version of Bob Marley's song, a young boy,
with the encouragement of three little birds, enjoys life and will not let
anything get him down.
ISBN 978-1-4521-0697-7 (alk. paper)
1. Children's songs—Texts. 2. Birds—Juvenile fiction. [1. Songs—Fiction. 2. Birds—Fiction.]
I. Newton, Vanessa, ill. II. Marley, Bob. Three little birds. III. Title.
PZ8.3.M39178Eve 2012
782.42—dc23
2012008533

Book design by Kristine Brogno.
Typeset in Coop Light.
The illustrations in this book were rendered in mixed media and digitally.

Manufactured in China.

10

Chronicle Books LLC
680 Second Street
San Francisco, California 94107

www.chroniclekids.com

based on the song
"THREE LITTLE BIRDS"
by
BOB MARLEY

EVERY LITTLE THING

adapted by
CEDELLA MARLEY

illustrated by
Vanessa Brantley-Newton

chronicle books·san francisco

Rise up this morning,
smile with
the rising sun.

Three little birds
        pitch by my doorstep,
singing sweet songs
        of melodies pure and true.
Saying this is my
        message to you...

DON'T WORRY
ABOUT A THING,
'CAUSE EVERY
LITTLE THING

IS GONNA BE
ALL RIGHT.

Run to the playground,
    laugh with my friends and play.
Three little birds,
    perch on the swing set,

whistling these words,
these harmonies sweet in the air.
Sometimes you just need to show you care...

AND YOU SAY,
DON'T WORRY
ABOUT A THING.

EVERY LITTLE THING
IS GONNA BE
ALL RIGHT.

Help in the kitchen,
stirring up delicious fun.
Three little birds
fly by my window,
chirping out loud,
they're reminding
us each day.
Everyone can make
a mistake they say.

AND THEY **SAY**,
DON'T WORR**Y** ABOUT **A** THING.

EVER**Y** LITTLE THING
IS GONN**A** BE
ALL RIGHT.

Lie down this evening,
wave to the setting sun.
Three little birds,
nest in the treetops,
humming soft rhymes
and lullabies, dreams to keep.
Whisper, settle now
sweet child and sleep.

Rise up this morning,
smile with the rising sun.
Three little birds
pitch by my doorstep,
singing sweet songs
of melodies pure and true.
Saying this is my
message to you...

DON'T WORRY ABOUT A THING, 'CAUSE EVERY LITTLE THING

IS GONNA BE ALL RIGHT!

AUTHOR'S NOTE

"Don't worry 'bout a thing,
'cause every little thing's gonna be all right."

Every child has worries—some big, some small—and my father had his share of them growing up. His young life in Jamaica was rich, not in material things, but in music, family, and friends. But the culture and natural beauty of his home had a strong influence on his positive outlook as well as his music. His song "Three Little Birds" has given hope to millions whose hearts have been lifted when facing the economic, social, and political challenges of today's difficult world.

For me, this song holds up one of the most important messages I want to pass on to my own three boys— that as long as we share our love with others, even if storm clouds gather, we will be okay. In this special adaptation of my father's uplifting song, I want to show through a child's eyes how he found hope in the world—how with joy and heart, and with those he loved close around him, he found the blessing of music to share with everyone.

Cedella Marley

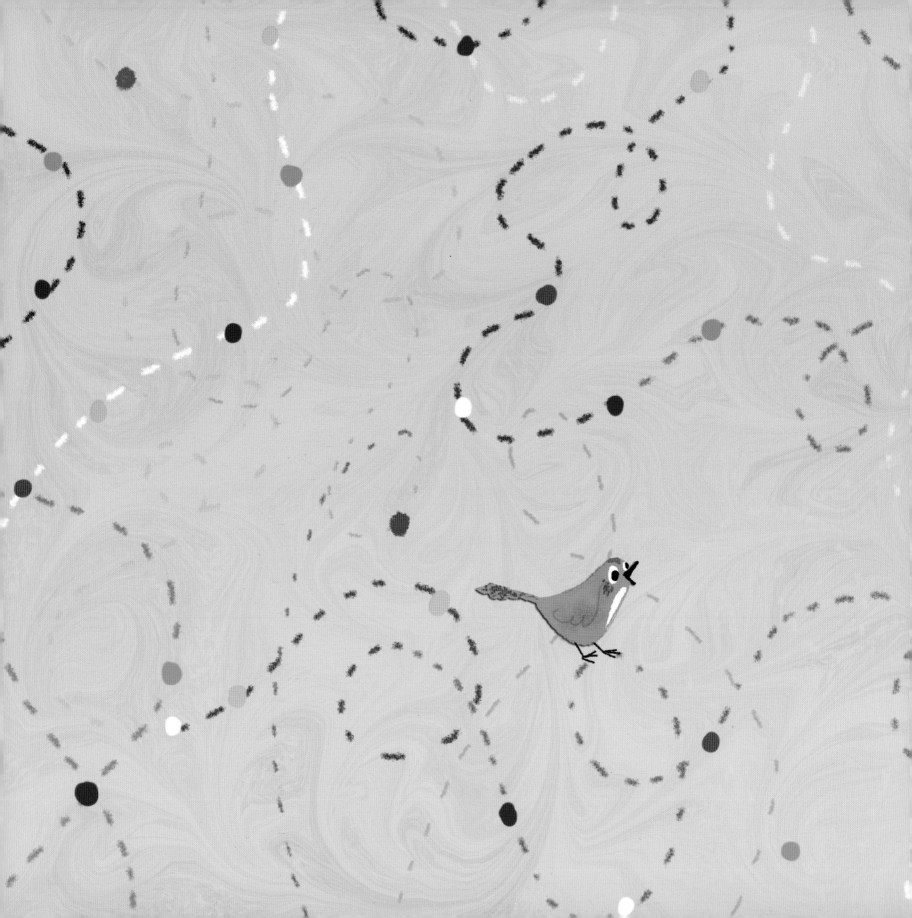